Dylan's
Dilemma

A gift for my most precious gifts,
Maia, Isabel & Sophia

Today was a special day for Dylan. It was the first day back at school after the long summer holiday. He kicked back his superhero duvet, stretched his arms up high and leapt out of bed.

Dylan looked at the clock on his wall and thought...

"I wonder what time it is? I can't wait to go to school and see all of my friends."

The long hand was on the twelve
and the short hand on the 7.

Dylan heard familiar footsteps
and the sound of whistling.

Daddy popped his head
around the bedroom door.

"Yay! Time to get ready!"
Dylan shouted.

"Good morning Dylan,
you're up early,"
said Daddy.

"Morning Daddy,
I know, I'm
too excited!"
squealed Dylan.

Dylan flung open the bedroom door and ran across the landing to the bathroom and picked up his toothbrush. Daddy followed close behind singing...

"Brush, brush, brush your teeth... swoosh...brush your teeth... swoosh...brush your teeth... swoosh...brush your teeth."

After his bath Dylan got dressed into his brand new uniform. He looked in the mirror, fixed his tie and was really pleased with himself.

"I've got to get a picture of you, looking all smart," said Daddy.

"Say cheese!"

Dylan did his best pose, while Daddy pressed the button for the camera on his phone.

"Great you're all set. Finish packing your bag and I'll see you downstairs for breakfast," said Daddy.

"Sure Daddy," replied Dylan.

Daddy turned to leave and it was then Dylan noticed he had forgotten his phor

Dylan knew he wasn't allowed
to play with Daddy's phone,
but he couldn't resist.

He picked up the phone
and jumped on his bed.

"Wheee... Look at me,
I'm Super D!"
he squealed, as he bounced
up and down whilst trying
to take a selfie.

As Dylan jumped higher and higher the phone flew out of his hand, bounced off the corner of his bed and landed with a loud THUD on the floor. The screen was cracked!

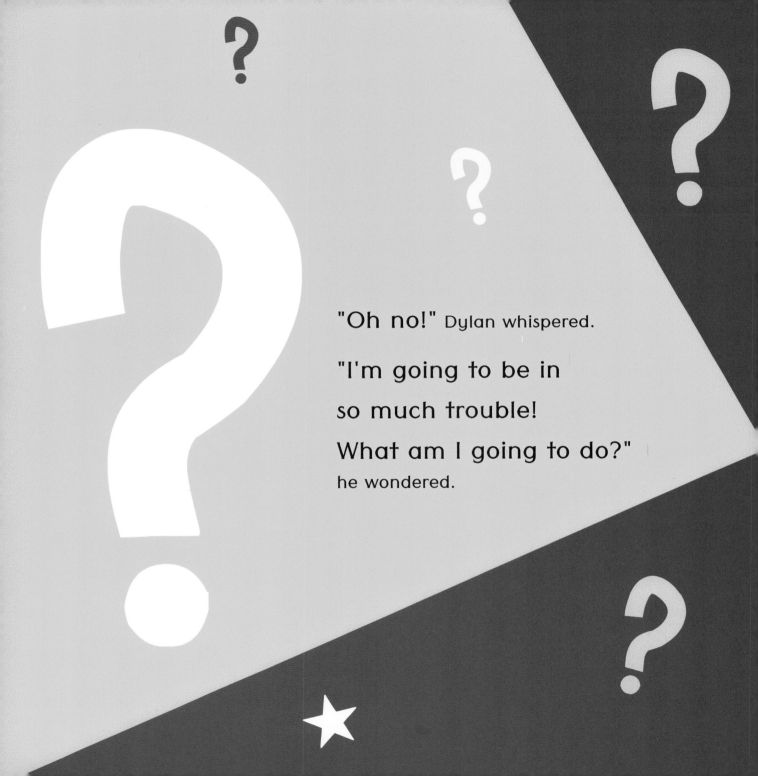

"Oh no!" Dylan whispered.

"I'm going to be in
so much trouble!
What am I going to do?"
he wondered.

Dylan grabbed the phone, stuffed it in his pocket and made his way down to the kitchen.

Daddy had made Dylan's favourite breakfast, scrambled eggs and toast.

Dylan sat down at the table, put his hand on his chin and pushed the eggs around his plate with his fork.

"Are you OK Dylan?" Daddy asked.

Dylan sighed and replied,

"Yes Daddy I'm OK. I'm just not that hungry."

"Not hungry? That's not like you Dylan," said Daddy.

Dylan took a bite of his toast but it just didn't taste the same.

"I want to tell my Daddy what happened, but I know I'll be in trouble. What should I do?"

"Time to go! Come on Dylan. We don't want to be late on your first day back, do we?"

said Daddy.

Dylan slowly climbed down from his chair, hung his head low and made his way to the front door.

Daddy helped Dylan to put on his coat and shoes.

Dylan looked up and said,

"Daddy, I've got something to tell you."

Dylan told Daddy everything that had happened and then gave him the phone.

Daddy took the phone, looked down at it and went quiet for what felt like ages.

"Dylan, first of all, thank you for telling the truth," said Daddy,

"But you know you're not supposed to play with my phone without my permission?"

"I know Daddy," said Dylan.

"So what do you think I should do?" said Daddy.

Daddy went quiet again
and sat down on the stairs

"Come and sit

down Dylan."
he gestured.

"Dylan, I can see how sorry you are. It's important that you listen to me," said Daddy.

"When I tell you not to do something, it's because I want to keep you safe or stop you breaking something!"
Daddy laughed and pulled Dylan close for a hug.

"I know Daddy," said Dylan.

"So this is what I've decided," said Daddy.

"Although I should cancel your sleepover, I'm not going to!"

"Huh?" said Dylan.

"You've been honest with me and I know you're really sorry. I love you Dylan," said Daddy.

"I love you too," said Dylan.

As they walked to school Daddy said,

"Let's grab some ice cream when I pick you up this afternoon."

Dylan looked up at daddy.

"You're the best!"

Printed in Great Britain
by Amazon